O9-AHV-519

54 Warrenville Road
Mansfield Center, CT 06250
860-423-2501
biblio.org/mansfield

For more than forty years,
Yearling has been the leading name
in classic and award-winning literature
for young readers.

Yearling books feature children's
favorite authors and characters,
providing dynamic stories of adventure,
humor, history, mystery, and fantasy.

Trust Yearling paperbacks to entertain,
inspire, and promote the love of reading
in all children.

THE FUTURE IS NOW!

Read all the Time Surfers books:

SPACE BINGO

ORBIT WIPEOUT!

MONDO MELTDOWN

INTO THE ZONK ZONE!

SPLASH CRASH!

ZERO HOUR

SHOCK WAVE

DOOM STAR

Mansfield Public Library

Mansfield Public Library
54 Warrenville Road
Mansfield Center, CT 06250
860-423-2501
biblio.org/mansfield

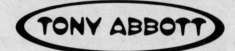

MONDO MELTDOWN

TONY ABBOTT

ILLUSTRATED BY KIM MULKEY

A YEARLING BOOK

2157

Published by Yearling, an imprint of Random House Children's Books
a division of Random House, Inc., New York

Sale of this book without a front cover may be unauthorized. If the book is coverless, it may have been reported to the publisher as "unsold or destroyed" and neither the author nor the publisher may have received payment for it.

This is a work of fiction. Names, characters, places, and incidents either are the product of the author's imagination or are used fictitiously. Any resemblance to actual persons, living or dead, events, or locales is entirely coincidental.

Text copyright © 1996 by Robert T. Abbott
Illustrations copyright © 1996 by Kim Mulkey

All rights reserved. No part of this book may be reproduced or transmitted in any form or by any means, electronic or mechanical, including photocopying, recording, or by any information storage and retrieval system, without the written permission of the publisher, except where permitted by law.
For information address Random House Children's Books.

Yearling and the jumping horse design are registered trademarks of Random House, Inc.

Visit us on the Web! www.randomhouse.com/kids

Educators and librarians, for a variety of teaching tools,
visit us at www.randomhouse.com/teachers

ISBN: 978-0-553-48306-2

Printed in the United States of America

Originally published by Bantam Skylark in 1996

First Yearling Edition August 2008

11 10 9 8 7 6 5 4 3 2

For Robert Boyd and Amanda Barrett,
our fab friends from Mega City:
Surf on!

CHAPTER
* 1 *

Ned Banks was running hard. He had one chance left. Only a few seconds. He whirled around and flailed his arms.

Too late! The shadow soared over his head.

"No!" he cried.

Swish! The fat brown basketball swooped in a perfect arc and sank straight through the net.

"Score!" yelled Ernie Somers, trotting to a standstill behind the basket on the Lakewood School playground. "The Ern-man powers it in!"

"My turn," said Ned, twisting his Cleveland Indians cap around backward. "The ball." He waited expectantly.

"Time out." Ernie made a T with his hands and leaned over. "I'm hot. Let's take a break."

Ned was hot, too. But he couldn't stop. He scooped up the ball and pumped it under his hand.

Blam-blam-blam. It slapped the blacktop, echoing against the school walls, as he took it out to center court.

Suddenly Ned leaned left, faked, and went right, his sneakers gripping the hot pavement.

Ernie's hands were everywhere, blurring, trying to stop Ned.

But no! Ned tore up to the basket, twirled once, and leaped. The ball left his hands, rose, and dropped over the hoop.

It tapped lightly against the backboard, circled around the rim, and—*plunk!*—fell off the outside to the ground.

"Oh man!" cried Ned.

"Now can we take a break?" asked Ernie, untucking his T-shirt. "I'm wasted. And soaked!"

Ned nodded as he struggled to breathe.

They walked over to a shady spot on the sidewalk outside the main school doors. It was early on a Saturday. No one else was around.

"No school for a week." Ned sighed. "This is the way it should be."

Ernie nodded. "Yeah, vacation is great." He was spending the week with his best friend. "So, like, what are we doing at school?"

Ned had to think. "Because . . . um . . . my dad didn't put the hoop on the garage yet?"

That was true. It had only been a few months since Ned and his family had moved to Lakewood. And there had been a lot to do.

A few months? It seemed to Ned as if a hundred years had passed since he'd lived back in Newton Falls with Ernie. A hundred years since his life had been normal. "My mom and dad say we just have to give it time. Can you believe it? *Time!*"

"They still don't know?"

"No one knows, except you."

Time! That word. It meant something different to Ned than it did for anyone else.

Ned traveled in time. He'd been to the future.

In fact, he was an official Time Surfer, the most honored thing a kid could be in 2099. That was the year he traveled to most often. That was the year his *other* friends lived in.

Roop Johnson and Suzi Naguchi. They were so cool. Well, of course they were. They lived in the coolest future imaginable! Along with Ned they made up Time Surfer Squad One, an incredible deep-space action team.

"The future is unbelievable, Ern," Ned said. "Kids do everything. They rule! Like Suzi, for instance. She's the best surfie pilot in the galaxy. And Roop, he's a real wirehead. A tech-freak!"

Ernie nodded. "Kind of like you."

Ned shrugged. "I guess so. It was my communicator that started it all."

The communicator was a little black box that Ned had invented so that he could keep in touch with Ernie. The communicator, or beamer, as Roop called it, just happened to open something called a *timehole* in Ned's new closet. A door to the future!

Ned never went anywhere without his beamer. He never knew when Roop and Suzi might call him on a mission.

Being a Time Surfer was the best thing that had happened since he'd moved. But almost everything else was terrible.

The first worst part for Ned was being separated from his best friend in the whole world. The second worst part was Lakewood School, where everybody from the janitor to the principal thought Ned was weird.

But the third worst part, and maybe the

worst worst part, was Ned's teacher, Mr. Smott. Ned was convinced that Mr. Smott was out to get him.

Mr. Smott complained about everything Ned did. Even regular stuff. Mr. Smott had stopped him twice just for grabbing the wall on his way out of the classroom!

"Stop that!" he would say, pointing to the shiny spot where the paint was getting worn away. "If everyone did that, the wall would be worn right down to the stone!"

With any other teacher, it would have been a joke. But Mr. Smott wasn't like any other teacher.

He meant it.

How many times had he written a note for Ned to take home, saying that Ned wasn't doing his best? That Ned didn't pay enough attention in class? That Ned was a day-dreamer?

Which he probably was. When all the other kids were watching TV or doing home-work, Ned was fighting smelly green aliens and trying to stop Vorg, a half human, half robot, from taking control of time.

Once Ned had even blown up a giant killer comet seconds before it would have blasted Earth. How could he *not* daydream about stuff like that?

"I need a drink," said Ernie.

"Too bad the school is locked." But Ned leaned over and yanked on the door anyway. It swung open. "Whoa!" he said.

Ernie grinned. "Water fountain!"

They stepped inside. The hall lights were on, but everything was quiet in the main hallway.

Ernie got to the fountain first, had a long drink, and stood aside to swallow. Then Ned bent over the spout and opened his mouth eagerly. But the moment he did, the stream of water dribbled to a stop. "Cut it out, Ern! I'm thirsty, too!"

But Ernie was across the hall, pointing at the ceiling. "This is weird."

Ned looked up. The hall lights were dimming, then coming back, then dimming again.

And there was a sound coming from down the hall. "Do you hear that?" asked Ned.

"Buzzing?"

Ned popped the basketball over to Ernie and started down the hall. "Let's take a look." They tiptoed past all the empty classrooms, their footsteps echoing along the halls.

The buzzing was coming from upstairs. Ned stepped up to a set of swinging doors that led to the upstairs wings. "These are locked for sure."

He pushed lightly on the doors. They swung open easily. "Or maybe not."

Ned headed quietly up the stairs to the second floor with Ernie right behind him. They pushed on another set of doors and moved out into the hallway, which led to more classrooms, including Ned's.

The buzzing and humming were louder. The overhead lights brightened and dimmed.

Ernie frowned and wrinkled his nose. "Maybe we should just go back."

"No," whispered Ned. "Something's not right." Quietly they crept down the hall and stopped outside Ned's classroom. Buzzing filled the air. Whenever the sound got louder, the lights dimmed.

The boys moved toward the door. Ned grabbed the doorframe and pulled himself up close. The wall just inside the door had a little shiny spot where the paint was wearing away.

Ned smiled to himself. Mr. Smott's spot.

They peeked into the classroom.

A man, his back to the door, was hunched over a black box the size of a small TV. In the middle of it was a fine blue beam. It was focused on a patch of shiny material. The material glowed.

"Weird science," Ernie whispered.

"Weird is right," Ned answered. "But who—"

The figure moved, and Ned saw the man's

profile. A smile was spreading across his lips.

"It's Mr. Smott!" Ned hissed to Ernie. "I've never seen him smile before! *Never!*"

Suddenly a sound erupted from Ned's back pocket. It was loud.

Diddle-iddle-eep! Ned's communicator!

A call from the future!

Mr. Smott swung around. In a flash, his large smile twisted into the most horrible frown Ned had ever seen!

CHAPTER ✳ 2 ✳

"What are you doing here!"

The boys froze in the doorway. Ned's hand was still glued to the wall.

Diddle-iddle-eep! Iddle-eep! sounded the communicator again. Still Ned couldn't move.

Mr. Smott stepped closer. "What's that horrible noise, Mr. Banks? And get your hand off my wall!"

Diddle-iddle-eep! Iddle-eep!

"Um . . ." Ned backed up, pulling Ernie with him. "It's—It's my stomach, Mr. Smott. I'm hungry, and my stomach is making noise."

Diddle-iddle-eep! Iddle-eep!

"What?" growled Mr. Smott. "You expect me to believe *that*?"

"Okay, it's not his stomach," Ernie piped up, pulling Ned down the hall a few steps. "It's his mom calling. That's it. She has a really strange voice. When she calls him, she says "diddle-iddle.' It's just a thing she likes to say. It means Ned should get home right away because—"

Ned stopped and gave Ernie a look. *"What?"*

Mr. Smott's eyes narrowed even more, and he frowned even harder.

He stepped toward Ned.

Voooom! The boys took off down the hall, leaving Mr. Smott and his big frown in the dust.

They flew down the stairs, Ned leading the way. He turned to Ernie. "That was incredibly lame!"

Ernie skidded around the post halfway down the stairs. "Yeah, but it created a diversion!"

The two kids tumbled through the swinging doors at the bottom of the stairs and out into the main hall again.

"Hey," said Ernie, slowing to catch his breath. "What was your teacher working on? A new kind of cappuccino maker?"

Ned shrugged. "Some kind of laser thing?"

"But why is he here during vacation?"

"Maybe he's always here. Maybe he *lives* here!" Ned shuddered. "Suzi told me that Lakewood School is still around in 2099. Maybe Mr. Smott is still here then, too."

Ernie made a face. "Scary thought."

They stopped outside the gym, and Ned pulled his communicator out of his back pocket. A coiled antenna with a blue ball at the top began to turn. *Diddle-iddle-eep! Iddle-eep!*

"This is a mission, Ern," he said. "We've got to find a timehole, pronto." He pressed a green button on the communicator and pointed it down the hall. The box hummed. "The pod! Yes!"

"The pod?" Ernie asked.

"The time pod that crashed here the first time I came back from the future. It's still in the closet!"

Suddenly there were footsteps thumping down the stairs.

"And Mr. Smott is still after us—let's blast!"

They ran down the hall and screeched to a stop in front of the janitor's closet.

"Follow me!" Ned jumped in, pulled Ernie along with him, and shut the door behind them.

Cleaning fluids lined the shelves. "Phew!" gasped Ernie, waving the air in front of his nose. "Thanks for showing me the smallest, stinkiest room in your school!"

Ned felt along the walls, groping for the back of the closet. Brooms and mops were stacked on both sides. He nudged buckets out of the way.

Ernie was banging into everything. "Um . . . could we have some light back here?"

Ned held out his communicator. "You

want some light?" He pressed the green button twice.

Zoosh! A ring of silver-and-blue light burst from the back of the closet. On the other side of the ring was a small bubble-shaped time pod.

Errrrch! Footsteps stopped outside the door.

"Into the pod!" yelled Ned. He dragged Ernie through the ring of light, shoved him down into the time pod, and jumped in.

Ka-voom! The pod's mini-engine roared, blasting the closet door back open.

The force of the takeoff pulled the basketball from Ernie's grasp and sent it flying. It shot out the closet door, dribbled into the hallway, and rolled over to a pair of shiny black shoes.

"Uh-oh!" gasped Ned, as two pale, white hands lifted the ball off the floor. A frowning face peered into the closet.

"We're outta here!" shouted Ned. Smoke filled the closet, the ring closed up, and the pod shot off into the shiny blue time-hole!

Ernie was thrown back into his seat. "Are we—really—going—to—the future?"

"Well, it's *not* the way to the bathroom!"

Ernie looked around at the strange worm-like tunnels shooting off in all directions. "This is incredible. A timehole to the future!"

"Yeah," said Ned. "It's kind of amazing. There's a whole world no one knows about!"

"Mostly in closets," muttered Ernie.

The pod zoomed faster and faster through the main tunnel. Ned checked his communicator. "In about ten seconds it'll be 2099, Mega City." For some reason Ned felt strange, as if he had forgotten something.

They blurred into turns, sometimes spinning completely over, then back out again.

"We must be doing two hundred miles an hour!" said Ernie.

"Three hundred, actually."

"I'm sure glad you know how to control this thing!"

"That's it!" Ned said suddenly. "Now I remember. I don't really know how to control this thing!"

Panic spread over Ernie's face. "You mean—"

Flump!

The timehole suddenly dissolved, and the little pod soared out over a magnificent, vast city of a thousand colors and a million lights. Buildings thrust up from the ground, twirling and arching in every direction.

Flying vehicles shot and veered all around Ned and Ernie in their tiny pod. Their tiny *out-of-control* pod.

"Don't worry!" cried Ned, furiously trying to find the buttons that might help him gain control. "Wait until you see the incredible stuff they have here, like the Sky Rink. That's where they play a game called bloogball. I've never found out how you play, but it's really popular. And wait until you see the reception we're going to get! All the kids in Spider Base will line up really straight and give us snap waves and—"

The pod dropped in a free fall, pulled up, curved left, then shot right.

"But what if we die first?" Ernie gasped.

"That probably won't happen," said Ned, ducking under the control panel.

"Probably?"

Rrrrr! The pod blasted between two orange buildings and headed for the ground.

Suddenly Ernie's eyes widened. "Donut!" he screamed.

"You mean bagel," said Ned, still fiddling under the panel. "Bagel means bad."

"Donut!" Ernie screeched again.

"The word is *bagel*!" said Ned. "Roop yells out *bagel* when we're in danger of being crunched to death. But don't worry, we'll make it. I just have to find—"

"No!" yelled Ernie. "I mean *DONUT*!"

Ned finally popped his head up over the panel and looked out in front of the pod.

Just ahead of them was a giant floating orange O. Blue and green blinking lights spelled out MEGA CITY DONUT MALL.

And they were heading straight for it!

"DONUT!" screamed Ned.

CHAPTER ✳ 3 ✳

Seconds away from a crash, Ned switched on his communicator. "This makes pods go crazy!"

Diddle-iddle-eep!

The time pod careened suddenly to the right, cleared the orange wall, and spiraled through the giant O.

"See!" said Ned. "I knew we were okay!"

Ernie pointed to something big on the ground. "Okay? What about that?"

"That's Spider Base," answered Ned. "That's where we want to go."

"*At three hundred miles an hour?*"

Buildings flashed by them on their way down.

"Four hundred, now!" Ned shouted. "But we'll slow down."

"Sure! When we crash!"

A hangar door flipped open just as they dived toward it. *Errrch!* The pod zoomed in and down a hallway filled with kids in shiny suits, who screamed and jumped out of the way.

"This isn't the entrance I planned!" cried Ned. Suddenly, ahead of them in the hall he saw two familiar faces. "Roop! Suzi! How do you stop—"

"Look, Sooz!" Roop called. "It's the Nedster! And he brought his pal Ernie with him!"

Suzi Naguchi watched in horror as Ned shot toward them. "He also brought a four-hundred-mile-an-hour time pod with him! *Jump!*"

In a flash, Roop vaulted into the air and landed on the speeding time vehicle. "Stop, pod, stop!" he cried, reaching around and

slamming the engine controls hard with his fist.

FLOO! SPEEEEE! The engine spat, coughed, and finally died. The pod skidded to a stop.

"Zommo!" Roop yelped, hopping off the pod. "Now that was some ride!" He grinned at Ernie. "Welcome to the future, Ern-man!"

Ernie gazed around at the smooth silver walls of Spider Base. "The future." He smiled. "I think I like it!"

Ned turned to Suzi. "So, why did you call me? Another Time Surfer mission?"

Suzi glanced at Roop and winked. "A surprise, Ned. But first, could we borrow your beamer for a sec?"

Ned pulled his communicator from his back pocket. "Sure, but why?"

"Just a little thingie I've been working on," said Roop, taking it. "Ernie, dude, I'll give you a quick show-round. Sooz, we'll be back in a nanosec." Roop ran off down the hall, with Ernie right behind him.

"You know, Ned," said Suzi, walking slowly down the corridor, "we've been doing some research about what happened to us on Centaur."

Ned stopped. The whole incident at the deep-space tech station known as Centaur rushed back to him. "You mean when the Klenn attacked us?" He remembered how shocked he had been to see creatures from the comic-book world of *Ice Planet Commandos* come to life.

Suzi stood before a gray metal door and pressed a button. The door shot up, and they stepped inside. "Just as we thought, Vorg created them from a picture of the Klenn."

"I knew it!" said Ned. "My trading card! The card that Ernie gave me with the foil-embossed 3-D creepy Klenn soldier on it. The card I lost."

The door closed behind them. They were in a laboratory of some kind.

"Vorg must have found that card," said

Suzi. "We figure he invented a special laser. When the beam hit the 3-D hologram at the right angle—poof!—instant holodroids!"

"Instant stinky alien holodroids!" Ned trembled at the thought of Vorg. "Anyone seen him lately?"

"No," said Suzi. "Cross your fingers."

"Slide!" someone screamed from the hall.

Wham! Wham! There was a double crash at the door.

Suzi smiled. "Roop," she said.

"And his latest student," said Ned.

The door slid up, and there was Roop, a scowl on his face, helping Ernie up from the floor. "I keep telling them these doors have to fly up." He rubbed his elbow and walked in. Ernie followed.

"Here, Ned-guy." Roop held out Ned's communicator. The little black box was different. A tiny red button stuck out of the side near the top. It was right next to the coiled antenna with the blue tip that Ned had found on Centaur.

"What did you do?" asked Ned. Roop

smiled mysteriously. Ned pressed the button. *Flink!* A small colored screen flipped up. It read: EARTH, MEGA CITY, APRIL 5, 2099, 11:22 A.M.

"The exact place and time. Excellent!"

Suzi pulled a small device from the back of her utility belt. It looked just like Ned's communicator, only it was green.

"Hey, now you have one, too!" Ned said.

"Sure," said Suzi with a big smile. "In 2099, every kid has a Neddy."

"A *what*?"

"A Neddy." She laughed at Ned's expression. "Well, who else were we going to name it after?"

Ned shook his head. "This is too much!"

Ernie patted Ned on the back. "Now you are immortal!"

Weee-oooop! Weee-oooop! A siren blasted throughout the entire Spider Base.

"What's that?" shouted Ernie. "Is there a fire?"

"Only in my heels!" Suzi cried, hitting little switches on her shoes. *Whoosh!* Tiny jets of flame blasted from each shoe. Suzi flashed from the room and disappeared down the hall.

"Suzi's got a game at the Sky Rink," Roop explained.

"What game?" asked Ned.

Roop pulled Ned and Ernie along, one on each arm. "Just a little something called—*bloogball!*"

Within seconds the three boys were flying the purple Time Surfer surfie to the Sky Rink.

"I can't believe it!" said Ned. "I'm actually going to find out what bloogball is! Is that the surprise you were talking about?"

Roop shook his head. "Later, Neddo, after the game. You just gotta wait." He chuckled as he cut the engines, pulled in the fins, and landed the surfie in a parking slot.

The Sky Rink was a huge round stadium floating high over Mega City. It had strange colorful designs all over it.

"This is incredible!" gasped Ernie. "Like something my little sister would draw."

"Kids built it," said Roop. Then he deepened his voice to sound like a TV announcer. "Just another wonderful example of how kids make the world a happier place!" He laughed. "Let's find Suzi."

They headed into the rink, up some sky tubes to the upper level, and out to the observation deck overlooking Mega City. People in shiny suits were everywhere. Kids snap-waved to Ned and Ernie and giggled at their clothes.

Ned adjusted his Indians cap and tapped Ernie on the shoulder. "Just be cool."

"Hey," said Roop. "There's our star!"

Suzi came running across the deck. She was dressed in a blue bodysuit with yellow stripes zigzagging up the legs and over her shoulders. On her head she wore a pair of silver goggles.

Ned looked for equipment that might tell him how the game was played.

"A bloogball is something like an orbot, isn't it?" he asked, thinking of the orbots on Centaur.

"Hmmm," said Roop, scratching his chin. "Orbots are nasty, deadly silver-colored laser-beam orb robots that try to kill. Bloogballs are sort of like orbots, I guess, except that they're not nasty or deadly or silver and they don't kill you."

Ned frowned. "No, really I've got to know—"

Bong!

"That's my cue," Suzi said, lowering her goggles. "Wish me luck!" She waved goodbye and descended a stairway to the playing field.

Roop pointed down a corridor. "Why don't you guys check out the snack deck while I nail down our seats. Grab us a couple fripples. With lots of sleeb, okay?"

"What's a fripple?" asked Ernie. "And sleeb?"

Roop made a face. "Well, a fripple is a . . . it's got . . . it's a . . . I don't know. A fripple's a fripple! Just make sure they don't burn them. A burned fripple smells real bad." Roop started for the seating area. "Stinky, like Klenn!" he called over his shoulder.

The crowd cheered inside the rink. In seconds the corridor cleared out.

"Come on, Ned," said Ernie. "The game's going to start." They walked over to a pod with wheels. An awning on top said FRIPPLES.

"We've got to find out what a fripple is," said Ned. "Besides, I'm hungry."

The crowd cheered inside.

Then suddenly the crowd went silent. In fact, everything went silent. Ned grabbed Ernie's arm. He knew this feeling. He tried to speak. But nothing came out. No sound at all.

Silence filled his head. It was as if his ears had been stuffed with cotton balls. Ernie looked frightened. He too tried to speak, but there was no sound.

Ned knew only one thing could cause this. He forced himself to say the word out loud. He had to scream it. "Vorg!"

Then everything became clear again. The crowd cheered and sound came back. The halls echoed again with yelling and laughing.

Ned grabbed his friend by both shoulders. "Vorg is here! He's right here! Only Vorg's time travel machine, the *Wedge*, can cause silence to take over like that. We've got to let Roop know Vorg is back. We've got a megaproblem!"

They shot down the hallway. Suddenly Ned stopped. Something flashed from the observation deck just outside the corridor. It was black and big. All angles, like a tank.

"The *Wedge*!" gasped Ned. He stepped out onto the deck, pulling his communicator out of his pocket. He brought it to his lips. "Roop!"

But before Ned could do a thing, a tall dark shape appeared next to the black time-ship.

Vorg! Ned trembled as the figure stepped toward him.

Vorg's forehead was studded with gleaming bolts. His head pulsed with red light. Steam spurted from vents on his neck.

He stretched out his hand toward Ned.

Ned felt a funny sensation in his palm. All of a sudden the coiled antenna with the blue tip popped right out of the communicator and flew across the deck and into Vorg's hand!

"Hey! Give me that antenna!" yelled Ned.

Vorg gurgled what must have been a laugh and disappeared into the *Wedge*.

Then it happened.

Whooooooooooom! Everything went flying off the deck and into the air!

The force of the blast blew Ned and Ernie to the edge and flat up against the outer rail. The rail that overlooked Mega City, half a mile below!

A black whirlwind, like the vortex of a tornado, began to spin in the air off the side of the Sky Rink. It was pulling everything toward it.

"Ned!" Ernie cried out. "I'm slipping!"

"Hang on!" yelled Ned, shoving the communicator in his pocket and inching over. "I'm coming!" He reached out for Ernie's arm.

But his fingers clutched empty air.

Ned watched helplessly as a tongue of black mist leaped from the vortex, wrapped itself around Ernie, and sucked him into the spinning hole!

CHAPTER
✳ 4 ✳

"Ernie!" cried Ned, watching his best friend in the world disappear into the swirling funnel of darkness.

Ned stared into the fierce depths of the black hole. If there was any chance Ernie was alive, he had to take it. He had to!

He let go.

Whoosh! In an instant, the whirlwind pulled Ned off the deck, and he whirled into the vortex.

Down he went, spinning around and around, amid the horrible noise, with blasts of freezing black air tossing him every which way.

All of a sudden something hit Ned in the arm.

"Owww!" he cried, spinning onto his side.

"Ned?" shouted a voice from the vortex. "Is that you?" Ernie appeared, tumbling in the air above Ned. "Sorry about my feet. I can't control my spin!"

Ned nearly laughed, he was so glad to hear his friend's voice. "That's okay!"

"Where are we?" Ernie yelled. "Is this some weird future thing?"

"I don't know!" yelled Ned. "Maybe it's a kind of time funnel!"

Ned struggled to pull his communicator out of his pocket. He hit the new red button and hoped it would still work without the antenna Vorg had stolen.

Flink! The screen Roop had just installed popped up: 2099, 2048, 2019.

"I was right! We're going back in time!" Ned cried.

Ernie reached over and grabbed the back of Ned's belt. "Let me know when we get there!"

The funnel swirled faster and faster.

"The place!" Ned shouted, squinting at the little screen. "It's not Mega City! We're going to—" He blinked as he read the year and the place. "Ernie, we're going to your house!"

"My *house*?"

"Newton Falls, your house, your room, same day we left!"

The swirling black mist around them was starting to get lighter. "Watch your head, Ernie! We're going to *laaaaaand*!"

KKKRRRUNNCHH–OOOAAAHHH!

They landed, all right. But not in Ernie's room.

They landed in a rock pile. In fact, it was a vast field of rocks. Black, hot rocks. The boys were alone. Everything was quiet. The vortex had vanished.

"My bedroom was a mess," said Ernie. "But not this bad!"

The air was dark and smoky and hot. The ground beneath them was black, as if it had been burned. It was like that as far as they could see.

"Ned," said Ernie slowly, "this is not Earth."

A hot wind blew across the rocky field. There was no sun in sight, and the gray sky was filled with mist and smoke.

Ned glanced down at his communicator. "It says Newton Falls, your street. Your house!"

"No way," said Ernie. "I've watched a lot of travel shows on public TV. This is no country I've ever seen. It's some other planet. It's some place that got blasted. Some kind of total mondo meltdown!"

"My communicator must have gotten bageled somehow," Ned said worriedly. "Maybe the antenna? I don't know. Let's find a timehole and get back to the future."

"And planet Earth."

Ned hit the green button on his black box. A second or two later he saw the shimmering ring of a timehole on a ridge nearby. "Bingo!" he announced, tapping some keys on the communicator's touch pad. "Space bingo! Just tap in some numbers and away we go!"

The boys ran over to the glowing ring and dived in.

Whoosh! The timehole sucked them into its glow. In an instant the boys were flying upward, holding tightly to each other.

"That was *not* Earth," Ernie said. "No way!"

Carefully Ned watched the time display on his communicator. The date advanced quickly through the years.

"Hey," asked Ernie, "what if we came up with an incredible theme-park ride like the ride we just had? We could call it 'Black Vortex Nightmare!' "

"Right," said Ned. But something was starting to bother him. Why had his communicator said it was Newton Falls when it wasn't? And what was that weird funnel they had been sucked into? What disaster could have made that other planet so smoky and black?

Too many bizarre questions, he thought.

Voooom! The timehole dipped and shot downward. The boys suddenly slowed down. The blue-and-silver light flashed. Ned and Ernie slid to a gentle stop in front of a gray hatchway.

"Okay," said Ned, getting up and brushing himself off. "Earth, Mega City, April 5, 2099, 11:35 A.M."

"Excellent!" whooped Ernie. "The exact time and place we left the Sky Rink! Suzi's game is probably just about to start."

"How much do you want to bet we step out right in front of the fripple stand?"

Ernie laughed. "The Black Vortex Nightmare is over!"

But when Ned pushed open the hatch, he saw that their nightmare was just beginning.

CHAPTER ✳ 5 ✳

Kraaaaaak! A jagged bolt of lightning zig-zagged across a black sky and exploded over their heads. Thunder boomed.

The scene before them was as dark as night.

Thick drops of rain pelted a cold silver street. Tall steel buildings rose into the black clouds in spiked towers and spirals. Sirens screeched and wailed in the distance.

Ned quickly looked at the screen on his communicator. "Mega City? I don't think so!"

Ernie peeked at the bleak scene, then

turned back to the timehole. "Definitely the wrong stop, pal. Let's try again. All aboard!"

But the timehole quivering in the air before them began to fade.

Ned held out the communicator and pressed the green button once, twice, three times.

The ring of light dimmed, sparked, and finally disappeared.

Nothing. Darkness. The timehole was gone.

"Is this normal?" Ernie asked.

Ned shot a look at his friend. "Something is very wrong here, Ern. Come on, let's see if we can figure out where we are."

Ned walked out into the rain. Instantly he felt cold, as a chill wind whipped up the long dark street ahead of him.

Ernie shook his head slowly. "We must have messed up big-time, Ned. This definitely can't be right. It's like a bad movie."

Ned pulled his Indians cap down low and walked slowly along the middle of the empty street. *But what if this* is *Mega City?* he thought. *Then what do we do?*

Streets stretched away in every direction. They were all slick, black, and deserted.

"Not a happy place," Ned mumbled to himself. "It's too . . . too . . ."

"Too dark and scary and cold and dark and evil and dark?" Ernie said, huddling against the rain.

Ned nodded. "That about covers it." Suddenly he stopped, holding Ernie back. "That smell!" He sniffed the air. "I know that smell! The Klenn! The bumpy green creeps! They're here!"

They dashed to the side of the street and went flat against a building.

Nothing. No sound. No *KLONK!* No *HISSSSS!*

Ernie jabbed Ned's shoulder. "Over there!"

On the corner was a round pod, about the size of a soda machine. It had wheels, and sticking out of the top was an awning. A man sat inside the pod.

"Hey, maybe it's not such a bad place after all. It's a fripple stand!" Ned said.

They ran over.

The man in the fripple pod was bent over the counter, rubbing it clean with a cloth.

"Excuse me, sir," said Ned. "Is this Mega City?"

The man didn't bother to look up. "Mega City? Ha! Is that some kind of joke?"

"Well, this is Earth, isn't it?" asked Ernie.

"What?" The man looked up at them. Suddenly his face turned pale, as if he was seeing ghosts. "Kids!" he screeched. "Run, before the hovercycles come! Get out of here! Run! *Now!*"

"But wait a second—we—"

The man pressed a button on the counter, and a gray metal wall shot down in front of him. The pod closed up, an engine roared, and the fripple stand shuttled off around a corner.

In a flash, the street was deserted again.

"Was it something we said?" Ned asked.

Ernie pointed to his friend's baseball cap. "Maybe he's not an Indians fan?"

Ned twisted his cap. "Impossible!"

A rumbling of engines filled the air. Sirens screeched and echoed off the walls. Suddenly three vehicles veered around the corner at the far end of the street. They were thick black hunks of metal, hovering about a foot off the ground. Purple searchlights poured out of each one.

"Hovercycles!" yelped Ernie.

But the worst part was who was driving them. As they rumbled closer, their features became clear. Each driver had a bumpy green face, thick, rubbery breathing tubes hanging back over its shoulder, and a long gun.

"The Klenn!" yelled Ernie.

"The evil Klenn!" yelled Ned.

The drivers spotted the two boys and gunned the hovercycles toward them.

Ka-jang! A flash burst from one of the Klenn and hit the street.

"They don't like us!" screamed Ned, grabbing Ernie and shooting off toward a low building nearby. On the side of the building was a set of metal stairs. A black iron balcony hung out from the second story.

"Split up!" yelled Ernie.

Ka-jang! Another blast screeched past Ned's shoulder. "I think they want to do that for us!"

Ernie ran up the stairs. Ned leaped up on a garbage can, grabbed the balcony, and lifted himself up.

Ka-jang! A third blast bounced off the metal stairs just behind Ernie's left foot. His sneaker started to smoke.

Ka-jang! Jang! Blasts exploded everywhere.

In a flash Ernie hoisted himself up to the top of the roof and reached down for Ned. They ran across the puddly roof to the far side.

Kank! Kank!

"The Klenn are coming up the stairs!" Ned shouted. He looked across to the roof of another building. "We've got to jump, pal."

Ernie looked at the distance, then at his friend. "No way. We'd never make it. It's way too—"

Ka-jang!

"Let's go!"

They jumped.

Wump-wump! In seconds they were down an escape ladder and back on the street, running fast. The Klenn were far behind.

"Whew!" gasped Ernie, pausing to catch his breath. "This place is dangerous!"

Kraaaaaak! Lightning exploded above them. A second later—*boom!*—thunder sounded.

"We lost them. For now," said Ned, stopping to look up at the black sky. The clouds thinned for a second, and he thought he saw a faint faraway glow. The Sun? *Was* this Earth?

Ned ducked down next to Ernie. Icy rain dripped down his neck. He didn't know where they were or how they would get back home.

"We'll get out of here, won't we?" asked Ernie.

Ned watched the shadows lift and fall against the high steel buildings. "Sure we'll get out of here," he said. "Or we'll die trying."

Ernie made a face. "That's not exactly what I wanted to hear. But I like the *we* part."

Ned managed a smile. "We can't wait for Roop or Suzi to find us. I'm pretty sure this is Mega City, even though nothing looks right. That vortex threw us into some weird time bagel."

But Ernie wasn't listening. He was staring into a building across the street. He pointed.

Ned squinted.

A face peeked up through a little opening set low in the wall. A hand was waving to them. "Help!" came a soft voice.

Ned looked over at Ernie. Ernie looked at Ned.

"It's a kid!" they both shouted.

CHAPTER
✳ 6 ✳

In a flash Ned and Ernie were across the street. They dived into the opening and tumbled onto the floor of a dark room.

The boy they had seen helped them up. Ned noticed that the boy's clothes were dirty and ripped.

"What's your name?" Ned asked quietly.

"Brin," the boy answered.

"Are you all alone here?"

A movement from the shadows made Ned jump. A figure came into the light. It was a girl. Like the boy, she was wearing dirty old clothes.

"My name is Terra," the girl said.

Ned looked around the dark room. "Wait a second. You two are hiding, aren't you? Did you do something wrong?"

"We're children," said Brin. "We have to hide from the hovercycles and the green creatures that ride them."

"Huh?" said Ned, confused. "This is 2099! Kids *rule* the galaxy in 2099. I mean, what happened?"

"We have only one ruler here," said Terra. "And he doesn't like children. He sends the hovercycles after us. He is the master of our planet. His name is—"

"No." Ned held up his hand. A jagged chill went up his back. He was afraid of hearing it.

"Vorg," said the girl.

Ned shook his head. "This is absolutely nutty," he muttered, pulling Ernie aside. "We must have gone way, and I mean *way*, off course!"

The room was cold, but it looked as if the children had tried to make a home there. Little candles sat on the floor, their flames throwing a small glow of light. Heavy black cloth covered the opening to the street. To keep the light in and the cold out, Ned guessed.

The cold came whipping in anyway.

"Okay, some basic stuff," said Ned, pacing back and forth. "My friend and I travel in time. We have a device that tells us exactly where and when we are." He pulled out his communicator. "But something's gone wrong, because what this is telling me can't be true. So we need to start at the beginning. This is the third planet from the Sun, right?"

Brin looked over at Terra. "Yes, but—"

"Okay, so this is Earth."

"No," said Terra. "This is Vorgon."

Ned frowned and shot a look at Ernie. "But this city. It's called Mega City, right?"

Terra shook her head. "Vorg City."

Ernie sighed. "I don't like where this is going."

Ned turned to Terra. "You mean Vorg lives here?"

She nodded. "In Vorg Tower."

Ernie wrinkled his forehead. "Vorgon? Vorg City? Vorg Tower? The guy doesn't have much imagination, does he?"

"He doesn't have to. It sounds like he's in control." Ned shook his head. "I don't get it. This is supposed to be 2099. But, instead, it's a future where Vorg rules? This is my worst nightmare."

"Thanks for sharing it," said Ernie.

Ned paced back and forth across the dirty floor. The candle flames whipped around as he walked. "Okay, something bad has happened here. This is the future, but not the future of Mega City and Time Surfers and Sky Rinks and Roop and Suzi. Not the bright future where kids rule, but a dark one. An unhappy one."

"Vorg's future," Ernie said.

Ned looked at him. "Vorg's future. But how?"

An icy wind swept through the room, flapping the black curtains and nearly blowing out the candles.

Ned trembled from the cold. "What's with

the weather, anyhow? It's supposed to be spring. Don't tell me Vorg controls the weather, too?"

Terra nodded. "Half of the year it rains. The other half it's burning hot, like a desert."

"Weird," muttered Ernie. "When did that start?"

"Since forever, I think," said Brin.

"No," said Terra. "My grandmother told me about it once. It was something big." She closed her eyes tight and pursed her lips. "A . . . fire? That's it, she called it a fire in the sky!"

"Some kind of war, maybe?" said Ernie. "Mondo meltdown, like on that other planet?"

"But this is all backward!" Ned exclaimed. "Kids are supposed to control things in the future. In another time and another place, kids like you—" Ned turned to Ernie. "Kids like all of us rule the world! We fly in space, play games, make decisions. It's incredible.

It can happen. It *has* happened. Kids can do anything!"

A tear trickled down Terra's face as she listened to Ned. "There is a group of kids like us," she said. "They're trying to fight Vorg for their freedom, but we can't get to them."

"We'll help you!" Ernie said, nudging Ned.

"But how?" asked Brin. "The other children live across the city. We'll be hunted down by the hovercycles. By the horrible green creatures."

Ernie grinned. "They're nothing but smelly Klenn. And Ned and I are Klenn-busters from way back. We haven't read two hundred and fifty-eight comic books and collected all the cards without learning a trick or two. Besides, it's like our old superhero friend Zontar says: 'Klenn are stupid!' "

Ned looked over at Ernie. "And I think I know just the trick we can use!" He stepped over to the wall and pulled the curtains down.

"Terra, you get up on Brin's shoulders. Ern, you hoist me up. ..."

Within minutes, two mysterious figures dressed in long black robes were hobbling down the windswept streets of Vorg City.

"Stop kicking my stomach, Ned!" cried Ernie.

"That means go left!" Ned whispered back.

The hooded figures rounded a corner and up a narrow alley. Ned knew where they were. Even though it had changed, it was definitely Mega City. He was sure of it. He shivered. *Mondo meltdown.*

They came to the end of the street, turned into a narrow side alley, and—*vrooom!*—hovercycles were thundering in from everywhere! In an instant the kids were surrounded.

A Klenn dismounted from his cycle, leaving the engine rumbling.

HISSSSS! A large burst of unbelievably bad-smelling air seeped out of the Klenn's wormlike breathing tubes.

"Oh, gross!" Ernie murmured.

"Shhh!" Ned gasped into his hood. "Let me handle this!"

The creature stepped over and spoke slowly, eyeing Ned from the top of his head to Ernie's feet. *"Kee-fa Vorg?"*

"Vorg? Selah!" Ned gulped as he spoke the words. *"Vorg po nichee rala siff!"* He bowed.

"Ugh!" muttered Ernie under his breath, as he listened to Ned use the Klenn language to praise the evil Vorg.

"E frenti-mara. Cha!" The Klenn snorted, waving his arm for Ned and his companion to pass.

HISSSSS!

Ned nearly dropped over backward from the stench of the Klenn's snort. A second later, the hovercycles roared away.

"That was incredible!" Brin exclaimed.

"Comic books!" said Ned. "They never fail!"

The kids walked on, from one street to another, finally coming to the center of Vorg

City. Icy glass skyscrapers cluttered the air. Iron bridges and cold steel statues of Vorg were everywhere.

"Poor Mega City." Ned sighed.

"There," said Terra, pointing to a small opening in a building. "The others live down there."

A few minutes later, Ned and Ernie were introduced to a roomful of ragged-looking kids. There must have been a hundred of them.

"Thank you for helping us to get here," said Terra. "How can we help you?"

Ned thought about that. "First we need to find a timehole back to our own world. Then we might be able to stop what Vorg has done here."

"There is a way," said Brin. "But—"

"No," Terra said. "Not that."

Ned turned to her. "Not what?"

"The pipe," said Brin. "The story is that there is a secret way across the city to Vorg's palace."

"And Vorg closed all the timeholes except one," said Terra. "It's in the Vorg Tower."

Ernie shrugged. "I guess it's the pipe for us."

Terra gave a nod, and a bunch of kids scampered over to one wall and slid a metal hatch aside. A black hole trailed away into darkness.

"You could get into very deep trouble," Brin warned.

"It looks like we're getting into very deep pipe!" Ernie sighed, squinting into the dark hole. "But, hey, we're on a mission."

Ned and Ernie turned to the kids and gave them an official Time Surfer snap wave. "Kids rule!"

The kids snap-waved back.

Then Ned and Ernie got down on their hands and knees.

And they crawled into the pipe.

CHAPTER
* 7 *

The pipe was cold, damp, and slimy.

"This isn't the funnest thing we've ever done," Ernie grumbled.

"Yeah," Ned admitted. "If we ever get out of this, let's definitely go back to this morning and start the day over right."

"It's a deal."

After a while a dim light shined ahead of them. "We're coming to the end," whispered Ned. He stopped at a grate covering the pipe. Beyond it was a room. A single light dangled from the ceiling.

"Uh-oh," said Ernie, looking through the grate. "A dungeon?"

"Yeah, or the basement of Vorg Tower. Or both." Ned pushed on the grate and it opened. The two boys crawled from the pipe into the cold stone room. It was cluttered with junk.

Ned searched the room with his eyes. "Stairs." He and Ernie picked their way through the junk and up the stairs.

"Ned?"

Ned reached for the doorknob. "Yeah?"

"Those kids back there, Terra and Brin and the others. They're pretty scared. Do you think they'll be okay?" Ernie asked.

Ned was quiet for a second. "I think it depends on what we do in the next few minutes."

Ernie took a deep breath and nodded slowly. "Then let's do it."

They pushed open the door together. It creaked slightly as it swung out.

Ernie tensed and held Ned back. "Unless Vorg likes his fripples toasty, there are some bumpy green Klenn around here. I can smell them!"

Suddenly—*KLONK! KLONK! HISS!* A troop of soldiers rounded the corner at the far end of the hall and marched toward them.

"Good nose!" Ned jumped a few steps into an alcove, pulling Ernie with him. They fell back into piles of junk. "What's this, Vorg's broom closet?"

KLONK! KLONK!

Ned tapped Ernie's shoulder. "Time to hold your breath!"

HISSSSS! A squad of twelve Klenn soldiers carrying very long, very wide, very jagged swords klonked by. They were going somewhere in a hurry.

The two boys jammed against the back of the alcove, trying not to be seen. The klonking and hissing faded away.

After a minute Ned leaned forward and took a sniff. The smell of Klenn wasn't so strong. "Come on, let's go up the stairs before they klonk this way again."

"Up the stairs? How do you know?"

"I'm not sure." Ned shrugged, heading up

the stairs. "I just . . . know. Besides, where else would a tower be?"

But there was something else, too. Something strange about the place. Something Ned couldn't figure out. At the top of the stairs was a set of swinging doors. All of a sudden—

Silence! Cotton-balls-in-the-ears silence!

Ned was stunned by the deep quiet. It felt as if the world was stopped, frozen in time.

In an instant it was over.

"The *Wedge*!" whispered Ned, ducking down and pulling Ernie next to him. "In the room at the end of the hall. That's where the tower is. That's where Vorg is."

Slowly they crept up to the door and stepped in. A huge iron machine stood in the center of the room. It soared up out of the ceiling, rising hundreds of feet into the sky.

"Vorg Tower!" Ernie cried. And sitting in front of it, sparking in the darkness, was Vorg's metal machine, the *Wedge*. It looked like a giant, ugly, time-traveling ax blade.

"I knew it!" cried Ned. "I—"

"You!" growled a voice from the dark side of the room. "You know *nothing!*"

Ned froze. Ernie's eyes went wide.

KLUMP-KLUNG! Something sprang out of the darkness into the glow of the black *Wedge*.

Ned knew that sound. He knew that deep, gravelly voice. So when he saw the rubbery, half-human, half-robot creature spring out of the shadows, he knew to be terrified.

Vorg. Part human, part machine. All evil.

Across the creature's forehead was a band of gleaming bolts. And his head pulsed with sharp bursts of red light.

In a second Ned remembered every detail of his first encounter with Vorg on Centaur, the tech station in deep space. He grew scared. Even so, he spoke: "Vorg, what have you done to Earth? What horrible future have you made?"

The creature's head twisted nearly all the way around. His black visor flashed at Ned. "Vorg's Earth. Vorg's future! Vorg, master of time!"

That was Vorg. Power-hungry. Time-crazy. Evil-to-the-bolts.

"We came here for a reason," Ned said. "We want Earth back. Our Earth!"

"Earth is no more!" Vorg gurgled through his neck vents. "You live on Vorgon now."

"It can't last!" cried Ned. "Kids everywhere will rise up and fight you. They'll kick you out! Armies of kids. Everywhere!"

Vorg sprang over to the base of the huge tower. "My future has no children!"

Vrrrrmp! A small panel at the base of the tower opened up. Inside was something shiny turning around and around. Waves of heat quivered up from it.

Ned leaned closer to see what it was.

A golden cone. The same cone that Ned had seen Vorg steal from Centaur. Now it had a blue rod coiling around from the top.

"My antenna!" gasped Ned. A thousand thoughts ran through his brain. "You stole that cone for your time machine. And you needed the antenna from me to make it work!"

Vorg's breathing vent inhaled and exhaled slowly. "Now I am master of time. Look around you. Your Earth has vanished. I reign supreme!"

Ned grew angry. "Your stupid future can't last!" His statement echoed around the room.

Vorg's visor blinked at Ned over and over. The room grew quiet. Slowly Vorg's rumbling voice spoke. It was as if he was speaking only to Ned. "My future began one hundred years ago."

"Ha," snarled Ernie under his breath. "No wonder he needs spare parts to keep him alive!"

Ned said nothing.

"My future began with a fire in the sky."

Ernie nudged Ned in the shoulder. "Fire in the sky—that's what Terra said!"

Ned still said nothing. He was trying to make sense of Vorg's words.

"It destroyed everything," continued Vorg, his visor still blinking in Ned's face. "It came with thunder more than a hundred years ago. It came with a flash of light!"

Finally Ned spoke. "What? What came?"

Vorg's visor grew bright red as he leaned forward. Ned could feel the heat of the bolts on his forehead.

"What came a hundred years ago?" Ned repeated.

Vorg answered slowly, almost in a whisper. "The comet."

CHAPTER
✳ 8 ✳

Ned staggered and fell to his knees.

No! he wanted to scream out. *No! I destroyed the comet! I saved Earth!*

But nothing came from Ned's mouth. His brain spoke to him instead. *Look,* it said. *Look all around you! The dark planet, Vorg City, the roaming armies of Klenn. All these are proof.*

Proof that Vorg had gone back in time to *change* the way things turned out!

KLUNG! Vorg started toward the *Wedge.*

Ernie helped Ned up from the floor. "Hey, pal, don't believe it. It doesn't make sense.

This isn't Earth. It's not Mega City. It can't be!"

"No, Ern," muttered Ned. "It *does* make sense. After we got sucked into the vortex, we thought we landed on some weird burned-out planet. Mondo meltdown, you said. But it wasn't another planet. It was Earth, in our time, just after the comet hit. And this is Earth—a hundred years later!"

Ernie was quiet for a while. "But how could he do that? It would mean that Vorg went back and changed what we know happened!"

Vrrrrr! The golden cone in the tower's engine continued to revolve. Sparks flew out of the top as it hummed.

"The cone," Ned muttered. "The cone runs the tower, and the tower is one big time engine! With this kind of power, Vorg went back and changed the past. He made the comet hit Earth."

Ernie frowned. Ned could see that he was struggling to think it all through.

"Ern, we've got to change things back."

"*You?*" Vorg quaked and gurgled. "You are tiny, insignificant insects that I swat away with a wave of my hand. I am Vorg. And this future is mine!"

"Oh yeah?" said Ernie. "Well, we know a lot of kids who want it back!"

Vorg growled an order at the top of his lungs. *"Fra-si hacho! Dort ahh—Klenn!"*

"Can't fight us yourself, can you?" snorted Ernie.

Immediately two side doors opened and a dozen of the bumpy-faced, iron-footed Klenn soldiers swarmed in.

Ernie grabbed Ned by the arm. "On the other hand, this might be a good time to leave!"

Ned knew Ernie was right. He knew it, and yet there was something he had to do. In a flash, he had it all worked out. And in a flash, he was in motion.

"Ernie, to the door!" he shouted. Ernie shot to the door while Ned faked left, turned right, whirled on his heels, and dived for the cone.

Thwank! Ned pulled the heavy golden cone loose and tossed it back. "Heads up!"

Ernie leaped for the cone, grabbed it, and bolted through the door.

Or where he thought the door was!

The walls, the tower above them, even the floor itself, began to quiver and crack open. Behind them was—nothing! Dark, open space, stretching out toward the stars. Nothing!

"Without the cone, the time engine can't work," cried Ned. "Vorg's future is crumbling!"

In a flash Ned was at the door, pulling Ernie with him. He clutched the wall as he swung out into the corridor.

The wall.

The wall!

The paint on that little spot of wall was worn away, down to the stone. A horrible thought raced through Ned's brain, but he couldn't believe it. He couldn't even think about it. He had to run. Had to get out of there—

Suddenly—*ka-blam!*—a door across from them blasted open, and two figures instantly tumbled in.

"Roop!" Ned cried.

"Suzi!" yelled Ernie.

CHAPTER ✳ 9 ✳

Roop slid to a stop at Ned's feet and looked up at him. "The Roopster, at your service!" Then he turned to see dozens of Klenn soldiers pouring from Vorg Tower. "Ned, you've really gotta start hanging with a better class of aliens!"

"Excuse me," said Suzi, grabbing Roop and pulling him up from the floor, "but we've got an army to escape!"

Ned blinked. "Um, right! Let's blast!"

Double-jumping the stairs all the way down, the four kids blasted through the bottom doors and into the main hallway of Vorg's palace.

Kkkkkk! The walls around them were wavering and shifting.

"Oh yeah, guys. Bad news!" said Ned as they headed for the front doors. "Vorg's time engine is on the blink because he doesn't have this!" He pointed to the golden cone with the blue antenna sticking out. Ned pulled the antenna from the cone and shoved it in his back pocket.

"This whole future is going to fall apart," said Ernie. "We only have a few seconds left!"

KLONK! KLONK! The evil Klenn were marching down the stairs after them.

"Or even less!" Suzi snapped. "Come on, the surfie's outside!"

They all ran for the main entrance.

Suddenly—*ka-blam!*

The iron door that led up from the basement blasted open. Ned heard the sound of many feet charging up from the basement. He squinted into the shadows and held his breath.

In seconds an army entered the hallway and stood before Ned.

An army, but not of Klenn.

An army of kids!

And at the head were two figures.

"Brin!" cried Ned, running up to the boy.

"Terra!" cried Ernie, dashing over to her.

Roop and Suzi stared at the kids standing in the shadows, wearing ragged clothes.

Suddenly Brin grinned big and gave Roop and Suzi the snap wave. "We've come to help you fight Vorg. Can you use us?"

KLONK! KLONK! HISS! BANG!

The Klenn army pushed down the stairs and into the hallway. They started toward the kids.

"Yes," said Suzi. "We could use some help!"

Suddenly Ned remembered something. "Don't forget rule number one—the Klenn are stupid!"

KLONK! Down the hall came the Klenn. If those bumpy green faces could have smiled, they probably would have smiled then. A hallway of little kids with no weapons. Too easy!

Ned quickly whispered a plan to his friends.

"Whoa," said Roop. "It better work, Neddo!"

KLONK! KLONK! The Klenn closed in for the kill. They edged closer into the shadows where the kids were standing. They raised their jagged swords high.

But just as they did, Roop hit the jets on his speed shoes, did an end run, dropped, and slid right past the ugly green aliens.

A moment later, Ned flung the golden cone in the air. It arced high over the heads of the Klenn.

Errrrch! The Klenn screeched to a stop. Their bumpy green faces frowned. They lowered their swords and watched the cone as Roop slid long and caught it, then tossed it to Ernie, who lobbed it back to Terra, who passed it over to Suzi, who shot it to Brin, who looped it to Ned.

The Klenn got confused and kept jumping for the cone. And when a Klenn is confused, its breathing tubes go limp and drag on the floor.

Every time they jumped and reached for the cone, they stomped back down on their own breathing tubes with their heavy iron feet.

The Klenn groaned in pain as they klonked all over the hall in total confusion.

"Zommo!" shouted Roop, taking the cone from Terra and sliding back down the hall. "What a team!"

Brin ran over to Ned. "You guys escape. We'll handle the Klenn."

"But you can't win this alone!" said Ned.

Brin smiled at him. "You taught us how to fight back. You taught us what kids can be, what kids can do. Remember?"

Ned smiled slowly. "You guys are terrific."

Suddenly—*kkkkkk!* The walls broke apart.

Icy winds swept through the hallway from the black space outside. Suzi ran over. "This can't last much longer. We've got to go!"

The kids rushed the retreating Klenn down the hall, whooping the whole time.

Ned nodded. "So long!"

Brin and Terra turned just before they headed upstairs after the others.

"Kids rule!" they yelled out. Then they disappeared through the swinging doors, the shadows turning blue and fuzzy all around them.

"What will happen to them?" asked Suzi.

"I don't know," said Ned. "Maybe we'll see them again—once we make the future right."

"I've got the cone," said Roop. "Let's beat it!"

Suddenly—

Silence! Numbing quiet settled in the hall.

"It's Vorg!" cried Ned. "He's getting away! We've got to stop him!"

"This way!" cried Suzi, running for the

main door. A second later, the four kids were outside.

Ned stopped short as he watched Roop and Suzi dive into their purple surfie. There, behind the purple surfie, was a bright yellow one!

"Hop in!" called Suzi as she started up their surfie. "It has your name on it!"

Ned read the side of the yellow surfie: TIME SURFER SQUAD ONE. PILOT: NED BANKS.

"That was our big surprise, Neddo! You're a pilot now!"

Suddenly—*whoosh!*—a dark shadow came zooming out of the sky toward them.

Ka-blam! Blam! Blam! The ground flashed and thundered in a storm of explosions.

Vorg's black *Wedge* coiled up to the clouds, hung there, and doubled back for another strike.

"Man the blasters, Ernie!" cried Ned, hopping into his flight seat. "We're on a mission!"

Vrroosh! Roop and Suzi's surfie lifted from the ground and veered off into the dark sky.

Ned hit the power control, and his surfie shot straight up after Vorg.

The battle had begun.

CHAPTER
✳ 10 ✳

The two surfies flew straight up over Vorg City and banked wide as the *Wedge* barreled up from below.

"Vorg's on our tail!" Suzi called out from the screen in front of Ned and Ernie. "He wants the cone!"

Ned twisted in his seat. The black *Wedge* was looping out between two tall spires and bearing down on the purple surfie.

"Hold on, Sooz!" cried Ned. "We're coming!"

Ernie locked the *Wedge* in his sighting system. He held the grip of the firing arm and squeezed the trigger.

Ka-chung! White flashes burst from the surfie's laser guns and exploded near the *Wedge*'s back fins.

The black ship faltered and bucked. For an instant it lost speed.

"Yes!" yelled Ernie.

In that instant Ned pulled up close enough to the *Wedge* to see Vorg. The silver bolts on his forehead glinted red in the light from the control panel.

Also in that instant Ned saw something else: Vorg's face—the part that wasn't metal—wrinkled into the most horrible look.

Was it anger? Pain? Was Vorg hit?

But the moment passed, and the *Wedge* was gone, spiraling away into the clouds.

Below, Ned could see the army of kids chasing the Klenn out of the tower and down the slick black streets.

"Vorg Tower, Ernie," Ned said. "It's got to go!"

Ernie nodded.

But no one else knew what Ned knew.

He'd been pushing the same thought around in his head over and over.

Vorg Tower was Lakewood School!

The moment Ned grabbed the wall on his way out of the tower, he'd known. That spot on the wall had told him. That spot, with its paint worn away after a hundred years of kids grabbing it.

He remembered what Mr. Smott had said about that spot on the wall. He was right. It *was* worn down to the stone!

Lakewood School! In 2099, it was the most evil place on the whole planet.

Ned shoved his antenna into the communicator. *Diddle-iddle-eep! Iddle-eep!* He scanned the ground below them. "There should be a timehole right behind Vorg Tower—" He banked the surfie around. "There!" he pointed to a small silver-and-blue ring glowing on the ground between two black buildings.

"Zommo!" yelled Roop from the screen. "Last one into the timehole stays behind!"

Ned gave him a signal. "Ernie and I have a little job to do. We're going in to destroy Vorg's time engine once and for all!"

Suzi gave Ned a signal back. "After that, head right for the timehole!"

"It's a deal," said Ned.

But suddenly—*ka-blam! Blam! Blam!*

Ned watched helplessly as the *Wedge* lunged for Suzi and Roop, the air thundering with blasts of laser fire.

A red flame burst from the back of the purple surfie. Black smoke shot out.

An instant later, the screen flashed bright with the image of Roop, his face twisted. "The future!" he cried. "It depends on you. Destroy the tower! *Destroy the tower!*"

Zzngh! The screen went dead.

"Roop!" yelled Ned.

Nothing. Only gray fuzz on the screen where Roop's face had been.

The purple surfie twisted, looped, and finally disappeared into the timehole. Vorg's *Wedge* vanished after it.

Ned struggled to keep control of the surfie.

"We've got to do it!" cried Ernie. "For them!"

Ned squinted, forcing back the tears that filled his eyes. "Blast the tower!" he screamed with a vengeance. "End this future once and for all!"

"I'm blasting!" cried Ernie. He squeezed the trigger.

KLA-BLAAAAAM! A huge explosion rocked the air, and an enormous plume of black smoke—black, like everything else in Vorg City—rose from the blazing ruin.

"It's gone," said Ernie quietly, as Ned swooped over the hulk and toward the timehole. "We did it, Ned. We saved the world from this horrible future!"

Ned was about to say something, but stopped.

Suddenly everything—from the crumbling tower to the plume of smoke—fuzzed out to gray, like a TV picture going bad.

Down below them, the timehole quivered, a tiny frail ring of light amid the tumbling darkness of Vorgon.

"The timehole!" Ernie yelled. "It's closing!"

CHAPTER
✳ 11 ✳

Ned jammed his foot on the thruster pedal. He pushed the engines, gunning them to the breaking point and beyond.

"Floor it, Ned!" screamed Ernie. "Get there now! Or we'll be left behind!"

KKKKKK! They dove into the hole at the very instant it closed up. It flashed around them, blurring and twisting.

RRRUNNNNNNCHH!

A moment later everything went black. And everything stopped.

Except Ned. He felt as if he was flying.

"Umph!" Finally he stopped, too.

His knees were pressed hard against his

nose. His feet were straight up in the air. His behind was hanging far below him somewhere. And every time he moved his head, it hit something hard. He hurt all over.

This can only be school, he thought.

And it was. The playground outside Lakewood School.

Ned heard a familiar voice. "When you dunk, you're supposed to let go of the basket!"

From the corner of his eye, looking down, Ned could just about make out Ernie, limping over from the school's front doors, clutching his shoulder and smiling.

Ned tried to move. Being stuffed into a basketball hoop was a problem.

"The surfie?" he mumbled.

"In the gym," said Ernie. "There's a timehole on the stage. The surfie and I stopped there. You didn't."

Ned nodded slowly, banging his head again.

Blam! The school doors flapped open,

and Ned craned his neck to see who was there.

It was Mr. Smott.

The teacher looked at Ned, a frown wrinkling across his forehead from ear to ear. He pointed at Ned and slowly drew his finger down from the basket to the ground. Ned got the idea.

He unwound his arms from the net, pulled himself up through the hoop, and jumped down to the playground.

He'd have to come back for the surfie some other time. He and Ernie began to limp away across the playground.

"Stop!" Mr. Smott said. The boys froze. Slowly he walked over from the doors, holding his hands behind his back. "Aren't you forgetting something?"

Ned immediately felt for his communicator. It was there in his back pocket. "Sorry, I . . ."

Mr. Smott swung his right hand around, and in it was a basketball. "Yours?"

Ned gulped. He looked at Ernie. Ernie gulped too and took the ball from Mr. Smott. The boys walked away without saying another word.

It was a while before they said anything at all. Finally Ned spoke. "They're gone, Ernie. Roop and Suzi. They're gone. Vorg blasted them. I can't believe it."

Ernie nodded. "They were the best."

Lunch was on the table when they arrived at Ned's house, but they didn't feel like eating.

"Hi, boys," said Ned's mother, getting up from the table where she and Mr. Banks were sitting. "There's a nice boy and girl in your room, Ned. They say they're friends of yours, but they can't seem to tell me where they're from."

Ned's eyes widened. "Boy? Girl? What? Upstairs? Now?"

"The young man keeps saying 'bagel,' " his father added. "Do you think he's hungry?"

Ned and Ernie blasted upstairs!

There, sitting on the bed, were Suzi and

Roop. They looked a little beat-up, but not too bad.

"You guys!" cried Ned, rushing over to them. "We thought you were dead!"

"Almost," said Roop, slapping Ned a high five. "But, hey, it was only Vorg. Besides, my mom would kill me if I was late for dinner."

"What about Vorg?" Ernie asked them. "He blasted you pretty good. We thought you were dead for sure."

"Vorg could have finished us off a few times, but he didn't," said Suzi.

"It was weird," said Roop. "I thought we were history, when all of a sudden he pulled back, shot off into a side hole, and vanished."

"But where? Where did he go?" Ned asked.

Roop slumped his shoulders. "Don't know. He's one strange dude. With that *Wedge*, he could be anywhere, anytime."

Ned nodded slowly. "Uh-huh," he said, pacing his room. Then he stopped in mid-step. "He's not in my closet, is he?"

Roop laughed. "If he is, he's fried big-time. Our surfie flamed out just before we hit your room. It should be an easy fix with some of your gadget stuff. Then we'll be on our way."

Ned scanned his room. His bookshelf was toppled over. Comic books and trading cards were scattered across the floor. Clothes were everywhere. *Yeah*, thought Ned, *the usual Time Surfer mess.*

"Sorry about the room, Ned," said Suzi.

He smiled. "It actually looks better than when I left." He was about to say something else when he saw the golden cone sitting on his desk.

Suddenly it hit him. "Oh no."

Suzi turned to him. "What?"

Ned stared at her. "Vorg isn't just any-where or anytime, is he?"

Roop stood up. "What do you mean, Neddo?"

"He's here," said Ned. "He's now. We destroyed his future. He'll want revenge."

Ernie frowned. "Vorg is here? In our time?"

"I can feel it," said Ned. "Vorg wants me. If I hadn't been there to blast it, that comet would have crashed into Earth. Earth would have shifted in its orbit. And Vorg would have taken control. Without me, Vorg's future *is* possible!"

"But you did stop the comet," insisted Ernie. "I was there! It was right over my house. That happened already!"

"Vorg is a master of time," Suzi said quietly. "He can change all that."

Instantly a thousand thoughts and fears came flooding in on Ned. And finally a single thought, a single fear. "He'll come back to stop me before I blasted the comet! He wants his future—Vorgon, Vorg City, Vorg Tower, the whole thing. And the only way he can get it is to come back for me."

"No way," Ernie said, shaking his head.

"Vorg can do it," Ned said quietly. "Suzi's right. He's a master of time."

"If he comes, we'll be here," said Roop. "Time Surfers stick together!"

Suzi nodded. Then she stopped. "Oops! I almost forgot." She pulled out a small shiny object from her pocket and handed it to Ernie.

It was a gold, lightning bolt–shaped pin. TS was engraved on the front. Ernie looked at Suzi, his eyes wide. "For me?" he exclaimed.

"Welcome to the crew, Ernie-dude!" said Roop, snapping the pin on Ernie's T-shirt. "Like I said, Time Surfers stick together!"

"Way to go, pal!" Ned said, patting his best friend on the back. Now Ernie was an official part of the team.

As Roop and Suzi briefed Ernie on Time Surfer details, Ned looked out the window, scanning the Lakewood horizon. It seemed like such a peaceful town. Miles away, far beyond the bank of trees, was the city that would become Mega City.

Or maybe Vorg City?

And Lakewood School. Or should he call

it Vorg Tower? Ned shrugged. It was enough to bagel his brain.

"Next week it's back to school," said Ernie. "Everything should get normal again."

Ned nodded. But he didn't really believe it.

Just then the door swung open. Everyone jumped.

"Hello!" It was Ned's mother. "I thought you kids might be hungry."

In her hands she was carrying a tray. On it were four giant bagels, each one slathered with cream cheese.

"*Fripples!*" yelped Roop.

"With *sleeb*!" cried Suzi.

Ned and Ernie gasped as the two future kids snatched the largest bagels off the tray and nearly swallowed them whole.

"So a fripple is a ... bagel?" asked Ernie.

"Bagel is bad," Roop mumbled between bites. "Fripple is mmmmm-good!"

Suzi licked the sleep off her fingers. "Well, we'd better blast."

"But where do you live?" Ned's mother looked concerned. "Somewhere nearby?"

Roop shot a nervous look at Ned. Ned glanced at Suzi. Suzi looked at Ernie. Ernie grabbed a fripple.

"Well, um, we're from . . . Ohio!" said Roop.

Ned winced. *Wrong choice*, he thought.

"Oh, my!" Mrs. Banks said, her face lighting up. "We just moved here from Ohio!" Then she frowned. "Funny, your silver suits. I—"

"Styles have changed, Mrs. Banks," Suzi cut in.

"Really?"

"A lot," said Ernie, nodding as he munched.

"Right, Mom," said Ned, smiling at his friends. "After all, it's the future!"

DON'T MISS THE
TiME SUrFeRS'
NEXT ADVENTURE IN

INTO THE ZONK ZONE!
BY TONY ABBOTT

Coming soon!
Turn the page for a sneak peek. . . .

Excerpt copyright © 1996 by Robert T. Abbott
Published by Yearling Books
an imprint of Random House Children's Books
a division of Random House, Inc.
New York

Originally published by Skylark Books in 1996

"It'll go like clockwork!" Ned Banks said into his personal communicator. "No problem."

Ned had been through it all a thousand times. He knew exactly how it would work.

"I get to school early," he said, leaning back on his bed and staring at the ceiling. "It's totally deserted, no one around. I slip into the gym, up to the stage, and into the timehole behind the curtain."

"Cool," came the response from the little black device in Ned's hand. It was the voice of his best friend, Ernie Somers, a thousand miles away in his own room. "Then what?"

Ned smiled at the next part. "I hop in my surfie and blast over to your house at a hundred miles a second!"

"Awesome!" Ernie said. "Can you pull it off without Mr. Smott catching you?"

Ned looked over at the big backpack sitting on his desk. It was stuffed with homework due the next day—the last day of school. His teacher, Mr. Smott, didn't seem to like Ned very much. He always frowned and sent notes home.

Worse than that, Mr. Smott always seemed to be around when Ned was near a timehole.

"Hey, what could happen? It's the last day of school. Of course I can pull it off. I'm a Time Surfer!"

Ned Banks was an official Time Surfer. With Roop Johnson and Suzi Naguchi, his friends from the year 2099, Ned traveled in time doing absolutely amazing things.

Ned even had his own bright yellow time-traveling surfie. For the past few weeks it had been stuck in the timehole in the gym. He had to get it out of there.

"When you get here I'll show you the brand-new foil-embossed 3-D Zontar card," Ernie said. "Ned, the dude is awesome!" Ned and Ernie collected every Zontar comic, card, milk cap, and action figure.

"See you in the morning, Ern." Ned switched off the device and turned out his bedroom light. *Like clockwork*, he thought. *No problem.*

But when Ned walked up to the front of Lakewood School the next morning, with the sun just creeping over the roof of the gym, it didn't seem like no problem.

It seemed like—big problem!

Hundreds of students and teachers and parents were swarming all over the school. The parking lot was filled with moms and dads dropping off their kids.

"But, what—what—how—" stammered Ned, twisting his Indians cap from front to back. "It's only seven-thirty. The school should be deserted!"

"The only thing that's deserted is your brain, *Nerd*," a voice said.

Ned whirled around. He knew that voice too well. It was his snotty sister, Carrie. She always called him Nerd.

"What are you doing here?" Ned asked, confused. He couldn't figure it out.

"Pretty dorky to be late the last day of school," Carrie said, ignoring his question. "Or did you forget the big concert? You were supposed to be here early to practice your part. Wake up, tuba boy."

"Huh?"

"Knock knock. Earth to Ned. Don't you know what time it is?" She flashed a fake smile, tapped her saxophone case, and ran to join her friends.

Time? thought Ned. Of course he knew what time it was. He knew more about time than anyone in the whole school. He traveled in time. He studied time. He knew everything about time, from when it started with a big—

Bang! The front door of the school flew open and a figure stormed out, frowning a terrible frown at Ned and tapping his watch.

"Mr. Smott!" Ned gasped. "Oh no! I'm late

for band rehearsal!" Ned was supposed to be rehearsing his part for the last-day concert, the big event of the year. He grabbed his backpack, made his way through the crowd, and hustled in the front door of the school.

Mr. Smott stomped across the hall toward the gym on Ned's heels.

Ned knew Mr. Smott hated directing the band. The real band teacher was having a baby. Mr. Smott had been asked to fill in.

Ned passed the open doors of the cafeteria. Mrs. Fensterman, the coach's wife, was helping a bunch of mothers and teachers decorate tables for the reception after the concert. Plates of cookies and brownies and piles of yellow napkins were everywhere.

"I told you before, son," Mrs. Fensterman said as Ned passed by. "Don't touch. It's all for later."

"Told me before?" Ned made a face. He looked over at the tables. Lemonade. Soda. Cookies. Brownies. It looked so normal.

It wasn't.

What Mrs. Fensterman didn't know—what nobody knew except Ned—was that a few feet away, in the kitchen's giant refrigerator, was a shimmering timehole to the future!

There were timeholes all over Lakewood School. In the janitor's supply closet. Behind the bleachers. On the stage in the gym.

Timeholes were everywhere. Ned even had a timehole in his bedroom.

But you had to have a special device to be able to find timeholes. A device that Ned had invented.

In fact, that was how it had all started. One night, just after Ned had moved to Lakewood, he'd been alone in his room making a super-long-distance communicator, a device he planned to use to call Ernie back in Newton Falls.

He'd made it with an old TV remote, some junk from a tape recorder, buzzers, lights, and other stuff.

But something had gone wrong. Instead of reaching Ernie, Ned had opened a timehole in his closet and beamed in two kids from the future!

"Banks, hurry up!" Mr. Smott called, pointing up at the clock on the wall.

Ned dashed for the music room next to the gym. He grabbed his big, heavy, monster tuba and ran back through the doors into the gym.

Bong! Ned tripped. The tuba sprang back at him, and he tumbled to the floor with his head in the mouth of the huge instrument.

This happened just as his sister and her friends came into the gym. They stood over him.

"See what I mean?" Carrie said.

Ned pulled his head out of the tuba and swept past them to the stage, stopping in the back row of chairs.

He glanced at a patch of floor behind the curtain. It *looked* like a regular wooden floor. But the moment he hit a button on his communicator—*whoosh!*—a blazing blue time-hole would appear there, just the way it did that first night in his room.

Tap-tap-tap. Mr. Smott hit the music stand in front of him. "Well, since you're all here now, let's begin with 'The March of the Soldiers.'"

The teacher frowned, raised his arms, and quickly began to swing them up and down.

Bump-a-dump-a-dump-a—Floook! Floook! The band began squealing and screeching and got worse with each note. It was all saxophones except for Ned. And he was the worst. Every time he blew into that tuba, it sounded like a cow with a bad stomachache.

"Stop!" cried Mr. Smott. "Stop this instant!"

He stormed from the stage to the gym floor. "Saxophones, down here!" he snarled.

Twenty kids rushed down the stairs with their saxophones, leaving Ned and his tuba onstage.

"Um, Mr. Smott?" said Ned, tapping his tuba.

"I'll deal with you later!" Mr. Smott barked.

Good, thought Ned. This was his chance. He slipped behind the curtain. "Ernie," he whispered to himself, "I'm on my way!"

That was the great thing about time travel. Ned could zip off to some cool place, have a great time all day, then come back to the exact second he'd left and nobody would even know!

The only problem was something called the Zonk Zone. Two people in the same place and time—that was the Zonk Zone. Ned had nearly been zonked once already. It wasn't fun.

He pulled his communicator from his backpack, aimed it, and pressed the green button.

Whoosh!—a silvery blue ring of light fluttered open on the stage floor. Beyond the ring of light a tunnel shimmered off into the darkness.

A timehole! Ned never got over the strange excitement of staring at an entrance into time. In an instant he'd be at Ernie's house, spend an hour joking around, and then—bingo!—be back before Mr. Smott had moved an inch.

He'd still have to play his tuba, but it was cool knowing he could see Ernie anytime he wanted.

Timeholes were excellent!

Ned jumped down through the blue ring, below the floor of the stage, and out of time.

There it was. His beautiful yellow surfie with blue fins arching up the back. It was sleek and superfast. Ned's little secret.

"But," Ned muttered, walking around the ship. Something was different. Something was wrong. The surfie wasn't where he'd left it. And the jets on the back looked like they'd been fired recently. "Someone's been here!"

Suddenly Ned heard a noise behind him. He glanced up to see the thick red curtains ripple, sway, and swing apart.

A face stared down into the timehole.

"No!" cried Ned.

✳

"Afterburners—on!" yelled Ned.

A burst of flame shot out the back of the little ship, sending a jet of fiery air up and out of the timehole.

An instant later Ned was gone, hurtling through the silvery blue timehole at incredible speed. The sides of the tunnel blurred. His face felt as if it was being pulled back into a silly grin. "That was way too close!" he said, setting the controls for Ernie's house.

Suddenly—*diddle-iddle-eep! Eep!* His communicator began to sound.

"Oh, no! It's Roop and Suzi, calling from the future! Sorry, Ernie," he muttered. "Our summer kickoff is going to have to wait. Future, here I come!"

He reset the surfie's controls and focused on the communicator's little screen. In the future everybody had a communicator like Ned's. In fact, they were called Neddies!

The years ticked by. A moment later the timehole dissolved around him.

The year—2099!

The place—Mega City!

Mega City! Vast metropolis of thousands of buildings, millions of lights, tens of millions of people. Tall towers soared up from the ground.

Mega City was home to Roop and Suzi and the incredible world of the Time Surfers.

Ned dipped the surfie under the Sky Rink, a floating stadium where kids played bloogball, the official game of the future.

The year 2099 was an amazing time. The motto was—*kids rule!*

But it wasn't always that way.

Not long ago, Ned and Ernie had discovered a different, frightening future. Mega

City wasn't Mega City and Earth wasn't Earth.

And it was all because of one person. One creature. *Vorg!* The name made Ned tremble.

Ned leaned over the side and spotted Spider Base, the official home of the Time Surfers. He pushed the control stick down.

Suddenly a shadow passed over his surfie.

"Intruder alert! Intruder alert!" roared a loud robotic voice in the skies behind him.

"Wha—" Ned turned to see a large cone-shaped flying ship closing in fast from above. A silver arm with a giant claw on the end shot out from the ship's great hull.

"Hey!" shouted Ned, trying to dip his surfie out of the way. "I'm a Time—"

Klong! The claw clamped fast on the surfie. Ned's engine suddenly went dead.

Rrrr! The giant cone shot forward, the tip spiraled open, and—*ka-thung!*—it closed around the surfie like a set of jaws.

Ned began to sweat.

A moment later the ship landed with a thud.

Rrrrr! The tip of the cone spiraled open slowly. Bright light flooded the chamber.

Standing in front of the light was a figure. Ned couldn't see its face. He could only make out its shape.

It moved toward him.

Ned could almost hear the deep, gravelly voice beginning to speak.

There was no place to run.

"Stop!" Ned cried out. "Get away from me!"

The figure stopped and tilted its head. "Dude, is that you?"

"Huh?" said Ned.

The figure snapped its fingers and waved its hand in a "Hi" motion. The official Time Surfer salute! "Hey, I do believe it's the Nedmeister!"

Ned couldn't believe his ears. "Roop?"

Flink! Lights went on in the cone. Stepping into the opening was a kid dressed in a silver Time Surfer flight suit. His hair was cut into a flattop with zigzags on the sides.

It was Roop Johnson!

"You!" said Ned. "I thought I was doomed!"

"Sorry about the weird reception committee," said Roop, tapping the cone's nose. "But we've got a very strange mystery on our hands. Let's get to the dome and I'll show you."

Ned followed Roop out of the cone into a large gray room. He recognized it right away as one of the hangars in Spider Base.

Kids and grown-ups in different-colored flight suits were scrambling everywhere around him.

"Ned!" shouted a girl from across the room. She ran over.

It was Suzi Naguchi, the third member of TS Squad One. She had a pair of goggles pushed up on her forehead, and her short black hair was tucked behind her ears.

"I just finished my homework!" she said, holding out a hand for Ned and Roop to see. In her palm was a small pile of black dust.

"What was your assignment, make dirt?" asked Ned, making a face.

Suzi laughed. "This dust used to be one of those." She pointed to a large metal canister that held fuel for rocket flights.

Ned's eyes went wide. "But how—"

"Zonk Zone. I artificially created a Zone in the lab to see if I could find a way to get rid of trash. I sent one of those canisters back in time to the same place and time it already was. There was, uh, sort of an explosion."

Ned stared at the black dust. "Sort of?"

"Zonk-o-rama!" Roop exclaimed. "That's the thing about time travel. Can be fun, could be deadly."

Ned nodded. "I gotta remind myself not to get anywhere near me, no matter when I am."